AF304702

Defoe
Abbott
Marx
Hardy
Melville
Montaigne
Machiavelli
Haggard
Chesterton
Cooper
Emerson
Joyce
Austen
Hugo
Eliot
Grimm
Stoker
Carroll
Christie
Maupassant
Byron
Molière
Schiller
Smith
Hall
Wilde
Engels
Garnett
Einstein
Fitzgerald
Hawthorne
Kafka
Goethe
Dostoyevsky
Willis
Cotton
Kipling
Doyle
Baum
Henry
Nietzsche
Leslie
Dumas
Flaubert
Turgenev
Balzac
Stockton
Vatsyayana
Crane
Burroughs
Verne
Curtis
Tocqueville
Gogol
Vinci
Homer
Widger
Tolstoy
Whitman
Busch
Darwin
Thoreau
Potter
Freud
Zola
Twain
Scott
Plato
Harte
Kant
Jowett
Lawrence
Dickens
Burton
Hesse
Andersen
London
Descartes
Cervantes
Voltaire
Poe
Aristotle
Wells
Cooke
Hale
James
Hastings
Bunner
Shakespeare
Irving
Richter
Chambers
Dante
Chekhov
Doré
Shaw
Benedict
Alcott
Swift
Wodehouse
Pushkin
Newton

tredition

tredition was established in 2006 by Sandra Latusseck and Soenke Schulz. Based in Hamburg, Germany, tredition offers publishing solutions to authors and publishing houses, combined with worldwide distribution of printed and digital book content. tredition is uniquely positioned to enable authors and publishing houses to create books on their own terms and without conventional manufacturing risks.

For more information please visit: www.tredition.com

TREDITION CLASSICS

This book is part of the TREDITION CLASSICS series. The creators of this series are united by passion for literature and driven by the intention of making all public domain books available in printed format again - worldwide. Most TREDITION CLASSICS titles have been out of print and off the bookstore shelves for decades. At tredition we believe that a great book never goes out of style and that its value is eternal. Several mostly non-profit literature projects provide content to tredition. To support their good work, tredition donates a portion of the proceeds from each sold copy. As a reader of a TREDITION CLASSICS book, you support our mission to save many of the amazing works of world literature from oblivion. See all available books at www.tredition.com.

Project Gutenberg

The content for this book has been graciously provided by Project Gutenberg. Project Gutenberg is a non-profit organization founded by Michael Hart in 1971 at the University of Illinois. The mission of Project Gutenberg is simple: To encourage the creation and distribution of eBooks. Project Gutenberg is the first and largest collection of public domain eBooks.

A Boy I Knew and Four Dogs

Laurence Hutton

Imprint

This book is part of TREDITION CLASSICS

Author: Laurence Hutton
Cover design: Buchgut, Berlin – Germany

Publisher: tredition GmbH, Hamburg - Germany
ISBN: 978-3-8472-1491-5

www.tredition.com
www.tredition.de

A BOY
I KNEW
&
FOUR DOGS
LAURENCE HUTTON

THACKERAY AND THE BOY

[p ii]
A BOY I KNEW
AND FOUR DOGS

By Laurence Hutton
Profusely Illustrated

NEW YORK AND LONDON
HARPER & BROTHERS PUBLISHERS
1898
[p iii]

By LAURENCE HUTTON.

LITERARY LANDMARKS OF ROME. Illustrated. Post 8vo,
Cloth, Ornamental, $1 00.

LITERARY LANDMARKS OF FLORENCE. Illustrated. Post 8vo,
Cloth, Ornamental, $1 00.

LITERARY LANDMARKS OF VENICE. Illustrated. Post 8vo,
Cloth, Ornamental, $1 00.

LITERARY LANDMARKS OF JERUSALEM. Illustrated. Post 8vo,
Cloth, Ornamental, 75 cents.

LITERARY LANDMARKS OF LONDON. Illustrated. Post 8vo,
Cloth, Ornamental, $1 75.

LITERARY LANDMARKS OF EDINBURGH. Illustrated. Post 8vo, Cloth, Ornamental, $1 00.

PORTRAITS IN PLASTER. Illustrated. Printed on Large Paper with Wide Margins. 8vo, Cloth, Ornamental, Uncut Edges and Gilt Top, $6 00.

CURIOSITIES OF THE AMERICAN STAGE. Illustrated. Crown 8vo, Cloth, Ornamental, Uncut Edges and Gilt Top, $2 50.

FROM THE BOOKS OF LAURENCE HUTTON. With Portrait. 16mo, Cloth, Ornamental, $1 00. (In "Harper's American Essayists.")

OTHER TIMES AND OTHER SEASONS. With Portrait. 16mo, Cloth, Ornamental, $1 00. (In "Harper's American Essayists.")

EDWIN BOOTH. Illustrated. 32mo, Cloth, 50 cents.

NEW YORK AND LONDON:

HARPER & BROTHERS, PUBLISHERS.

Copyright, 1898, by Harper & Brothers.

[p iv]

TO

MARK TWAIN
THE CREATOR OF
TOM SAWYER
ONE OF THE BEST BOYS
I EVER KNEW

[p v]
May the light of some morning skies
In days when the sun knew how to rise,
Stay with my spirit until I go
To be the boy that I used to know.

H. C. Bunner, in "Rowen."

[p ix]
INTRODUCTORY NOTE

The papers upon which this volume is founded — published here by the courtesy of The Century Company — appeared originally in the columns of *St. Nicholas*. They have been reconstructed and rearranged, and not a little new matter has been added.

The portraits are all from life. That of The Boy's Scottish grandfather, facing page 20, is from a photograph by Sir David Brewster, taken in St. Andrews in 1846 or 1847. The subject sat in his own garden, blinking at the sun for many minutes, in front of the camera, when tradition says that his patience became exhausted and the artist permitted him to move. The Boy distinctly remembers the great interest the picture excited when it first reached this country.

Behind the tree in the extreme left of the view of The Boy's Scottish-American grandfather's house in New York, facing page 22, may be seen a portion of the home of Mr. Thomas Bailey Aldrich, in 1843 or 1844, some years earlier than the period of "The [p x] Story of a Bad Boy." Warm and constant friends — as men — for upwards of a quarter of a century, it is rather a curious coincidence that the boys — as boys — should have been near neighbors, although they did not know each other then, nor do they remember the fact.

The histories of "A Boy I Knew" and the "Four Dogs" are absolutely true, from beginning to end; nothing has been invented; no incident has been palliated or elaborated. The author hopes that the volume may interest the boys and girls he does not know as much as it has interested him. He has read it more than once; he has laughed over it, and he has cried over it; it has appealed to him in a peculiar way. But then, he knew The Dogs, and he knew The Boy!

L. H.

[p 1]
A BOY I KNEW

[p 3]
A BOY I KNEW

He was not a very good boy, or a very bad boy, or a very bright boy, or an unusual boy in any way. He was just a boy; and very often he forgets that he is not a boy now. Whatever there may be about The Boy that is commendable he owes to his father and to his mother; and he feels that he should not be held responsible for that.

His mother was the most generous and the most unselfish of human beings. She was always thinking of somebody else—always doing for others. To her it was blessèd to give, and it was not very pleasant to receive. When she bought anything, The Boy's stereotyped query was, "Who is to have it?" When anything was bought for her, her own invariable remark was, "What on earth shall I do with it?" When The Boy came to her, one summer morning, she looked upon him as a gift from Heaven; and when she was told that it *was* a boy, and not a bad-looking or a bad-conditioned boy, her [p 4] first words were, "What on earth shall I do with it?"

She found plenty "to do with it" before she got through with it, more than forty years afterwards; and The Boy has every reason to believe that she never regretted the gift. Indeed, she once told him, late in her life, that he had never made her cry! What better benediction can a boy have than that?

The Boy's father was a scholar, and a ripe and good one. Self-made and self-taught, he began the serious struggle of life when he was merely a boy himself; and reading, and writing, and spelling, and languages, and mathematics came to him by nature. He acquired by slow degrees a fine library, and out of it a vast amount of information. He never bought a book that he did not read, and he never read a book unless he considered it worth buying and worth keeping. Languages and mathematics were his particular delight. When he was tired he rested himself by the solving of a geometrical prob-

lem. He studied his Bible in Latin, in Greek, in Hebrew, and he had
no small smattering of Sanskrit. His chief recreation, on a Sunday
afternoon or on a long summer evening, was a walk with The Boy
among the Hudson River docks, when the business of the day, or
the week, was over and the ship was left in charge of some old
quartermaster or third mate. To these sailors the father would talk
in each sailor's own tongue, whether [p 5]
it were Dutch or Danish, Spanish or Swedish, Russian or Prussian,
or a *patois* of something else, always to the great wonderment of The
Boy, who to this day, after many years of foreign travel, knows little
more of French than "*Combien?*" and little more of Italian than
"*Troppo caro.*" Why none of these qualities of mind came to The Boy
by direct descent he does not know. He only knows that he did
inherit from his parent, in an intellectual way, a sense of humor, a
love for books—as books—and a certain respect for the men by
whom books are written.

THE BOY'S MOTHER

It seemed to The Boy that his father knew everything. Any question upon any subject was sure to bring a prompt, intelligent, and intelligible answer; and, usually, an answer followed by a question, on the father's part, which made The Boy think the matter out for himself.

The Boy was always a little bit afraid of his father, while he loved and respected him. He believed everything his father told him, because his father never fooled him but once, and that was about Santa Claus!

When his father said, "Do this," it was done. When his father told him to go or to come, he went or he came. And yet he never felt the weight of his father's hand, except in the way of kindness; and, as he looks back upon his boyhood and his manhood, he cannot recall an angry or a hasty word or a rebuke [p 6]
that was not merited and kindly bestowed. His father, like the true Scotchman he was, never praised him; but he never blamed him — except for cause.

The Boy has no recollection of his first tooth, but he remembers his first toothache as distinctly as he remembers his latest; and he could not quite understand *then* why, when The Boy cried over that raging molar, the father walked the floor and seemed to suffer from it even more than did The Boy; or why, when The Boy had a sore throat, the father always had symptoms of bronchitis or quinsy.

The father, alas! did not live long enough to find out whether The Boy was to amount to much or not; and while The Boy is proud of the fact that he is his father's son, he would be prouder still if he could think that he had done something to make his father proud of *him*.

From his father The Boy received many things besides birth and education; many things better than pocket-money or a fixed sum per annum; but, best of all, the father taught The Boy never to cut a string. The Boy has pulled various cords during his uneventful life, but he has untied them all. Some of the knots have been difficult and perplexing, and the contents of the bundles, generally, have been of little import when they have been revealed; but he saved the strings unbroken, and invariably he has found those strings of great help to him in the proper [p 7]
fastening of the next package he has had occasion to send away.

ST. JOHN'S CHAPEL AND PARK

The father had that strong sense of humor which Dr. Johnson—who had no sense of humor whatever—denied to all Scotchmen. No surgical operation was necessary to put one of Sydney Smith's jokes into the father's head, or to keep it there. His own jokes were as original as they were harmless, and they were as delightful as was his quick appreciation of the jokes of other persons.

A long siege with a certain bicuspid had left The Boy, one early spring day, with a broken spirit and a swollen face. The father was going, that morning, to attend the funeral of his old friend, Dr. McPherson, and, before he left the house, he asked The Boy what should be brought back to him as a solace. Without hesitation, a brick of maple sugar was demanded—a very strange request, certainly, from a person in that peculiar condition of invalidism, and one which appealed strongly to the father's own sense of the ridiculous.

When the father returned, at dinner-time, he carried the brick, enveloped in many series of papers, beginning with the coarsest kind and ending with the finest kind; and each of the wrappers was fas-

tened with its own particular bit of cord or ribbon, all of them tied
in the hardest of hard knots. The process of disentanglement was
long and laborious, but it was [p 8]
persistently performed; and when the brick was revealed, lo! it was
just a brick—not of maple sugar, but a plain, ordinary, red-clay,
building brick which he had taken from some pile of similar bricks
on his way up town. The disappointment was not very bitter, for
The Boy knew that something else was coming; and he realized that
it was the First of April and that he had been April-fooled! The
something else, he remembers, was that most amusing of all amusing books, *Phœnixiana*, then just published, and over it he forgot his
toothache, but not his maple sugar. All this happened when he was
about twelve years of age, and he has ever since associated
"Squibob" with the sweet sap of the maple, never with raging teeth.
It was necessary, however, to get even with the father, not an easy
matter, as The Boy well knew; and he consulted his uncle John, who
advised patient waiting. The father, he said, was absolutely devoted
to *The Commercial Advertiser*, which he read every day from frontis-
piece to end, market reports, book notices, obituary notices, adver-
tisements, and all; and if The Boy could hold himself in for a whole
year his uncle John thought it would be worth it. *The Commercial
Advertiser* of that date was put safely away for a twelvemonth, and
on the First of April next it was produced, carefully folded and
properly dampened, and was placed by the side [p 9]
of the father's plate; the mother and the son making no remark, but
eagerly awaiting the result. The journal was vigorously scanned; no
item of news or of business import was missed until the reader
came to the funeral announcements on the third page. Then he
looked at the top of the paper, through his spectacles, and then he
looked, over his spectacles, at The Boy; and he made but one obser-
vation. The subject was never referred to afterwards between them.
But he looked at the date of the paper, and he looked at The Boy;
and he said: "My son, I see that old Dr. McPherson is dead again!"

THE BOY'S UNCLE JOHN

The Boy was red-headed and long-nosed, even from the beginning — a shy, introspective, self-conscious little boy, made peculiarly
familiar with his personal defects by constant remarks that his hair
was red and that his nose *was* long. At school, for years, he was
known familiarly as "Rufus," "Red-Head," "Carrot-Top," or "Nos-
ey," and at home it was almost as bad.

His mother, married at nineteen, was the eldest of a family of nine
children, and many of The Boy's aunts and uncles were but a few
years his senior, and were his daily, familiar companions. He was
the only member of his own generation for a long time. There was a
constant fear, upon the part of the elders, that he was likely to be
spoiled, and consequently the rod of verbal castigation was rarely
spared. He was never praised, nor petted, nor coddled; and he was
[p 10]
taught to look upon himself as a youth hairily and nasally deformed
and mentally of but little wit. He was always falling down, or drop-

ping things. He was always getting into the way, and he could not learn to spell correctly or to cipher at all. He was never in his mother's way, however, and he was never made to feel so. But nobody except The Boy knows of the agony which the rest of the family, unconsciously, and with no thought of hurting his feelings, caused him by the fun they poked at his nose, at his fiery locks, and at his unhandiness. He fancied that passers-by pitied him as he walked or played in the streets, and he sincerely pitied himself as a youth destined to grow up into an awkward, tactless, stupid man, at whom the world would laugh so long as his life lasted.

An unusual and unfortunate accident to his nose when he was eight or ten years old served to accentuate his unhappiness. The young people were making molasses candy one night in the kitchen of his maternal grandfather's house — the aunts and the uncles, some of the neighbors' children, and The Boy — and the half of a lemon, used for flavoring purposes, was dropped as it was squeezed by careless hands — very likely The Boy's own — into the boiling syrup. It was fished out and put, still full of the syrup, upon a convenient saucer, where it remained, an exceedingly fragrant object. After the odor had [p 11]

been inhaled by one or two of the party, The Boy was tempted to "take a smell of it"; when an uncle, boylike, ducked the luckless nose into the still simmering lemonful. The result was terrible. Red-hot sealing-wax could not have done more damage to the tender, sensitive feature.

THE BOY IN KILTS

The Boy carried his nose in a sling for many weeks, and the bandage, naturally, twisted the nose to one side. It did not recover its natural tint for a long time, and the poor little heart was nearly broken at the thought of the fresh disfigurement. The Boy felt that he had not only an unusually long nose, but a nose that was crooked and would always be as red as his hair.

He does not remember what was done to his uncle. But the uncle was for half a century The Boy's best and most faithful of friends. And The Boy forgave him long, long ago.

The Boy's first act of self-reliance and of conscious self-dependence was a very happy moment in his young life; and it consisted in his being able to step over the nursery fender, all alone, and to toast his own shins thereby, without falling into the fire. His first realization of "getting big" came to him about the same time, and with a mingled shock of pain and pleasure, when he discovered that he could not walk under the high kitchen-table without bumping his head. He tried it very often before he learned [p 12]
to go around that article of furniture, on his way from the clothes-rack, which was his tent when he camped out on rainy days, to the sink, which was his oasis in the desert of the basement floor. This kitchen was a favorite playground of The Boy, and about that kitchen-table centre many of the happiest of his early reminiscences. Ann Hughes, the cook, was very good to The Boy. She told him stories, and taught him riddles, all about a certain "Miss Netticoat," who wore a white petticoat, and who had a red nose, and about whom there still lingers a queer, contradictory legend to the effect that "the longer she stands the shorter she grows." The Boy always felt that, on account of her nose, there was a peculiar bond of sympathy between little Miss Netticoat and himself.
As he was all boy in his games, he would never cherish anything but a boy-doll, generally a Highlander, in kilts and with a glengarry, that came off! And although he became foreman of a juvenile hook-and-ladder company before he was five, and would not play with girls at all, he had one peculiar feminine weakness. His grand passion was washing and ironing. And Ann Hughes used to let him do all the laundry-work connected with the wash-rags and his own pocket-handkerchiefs, into which, regularly, every Wednesday, he burned little brown holes with the toy flat-iron, which *would* get too hot. But [p 13]
Johnny Robertson and Joe Stuart and the other boys, and even the uncles and the aunts, never knew anything about that—unless Ann Hughes gave it away!

THE BOY PROMOTED TO TROUSERS

The Boy seems to have developed, very early in life, a fondness for
new clothes—a fondness which his wife sometimes thinks he has
quite outgrown. It is recorded that almost his first plainly spoken
words were "Coat and hat," uttered upon his promotion into a
more boyish apparel than the caps and frocks of his infancy. And he
remembers very distinctly his first pair of long trousers, and the

impression they made upon him, in more ways than one. They were a black-and-white check, and to them was attached that especially manly article, the suspender. They were originally worn in celebration of the birth of the New Year, in 1848 or 1849, and The Boy went to his father's store in Hudson Street, New York, to exhibit them on the next business-day thereafter. Naturally they excited much comment, and were the subject of sincere congratulation. And two young clerks of his father, The Boy's uncles, amused themselves, and The Boy, by playing with him a then popular game called "Squails." They put The Boy, seated, on a long counter, and they slid him, backward and forward between them, with great skill and no little force. But, before the championship was decided, The Boy's mother broke [p 14]
up the game, boxed the ears of the players, and carried the human disk home in disgrace; pressing as she went, and not very gently, the seat of The Boy's trousers with the palm of her hand!

He remembers nothing more about the trousers, except the fact that for a time he was allowed to appear in them on Sundays and holidays only, and that he was deeply chagrined at having to go back to knickerbockers at school and at play.

The Boy's first boots were of about this same era. They were what were then known as "Wellingtons," and they had legs. The legs had red leather tops, as was the fashion in those days, and the boots were pulled on with straps. They were always taken off with the aid of the boot-jack of The Boy's father, although they could have been removed much more easily without the use of that instrument. Great was the day when The Boy first wore his first boots to school; and great his delight at the sensation he thought they created when they were exhibited in the primary department.

The Boy's first school was a dame's school, kept by a Miss or Mrs. Harrison, in Harrison Street, near the Hudson Street house in which he was born. He was the smallest child in the establishment, and probably a pet of the larger girls, for he remembers going home to his mother in tears, because one of them had kissed him behind the class-room door. [p 15]
He saw her often, in later years, but she never tried to do it again!

"CRIED, BECAUSE HE HAD BEEN KISSED"

At that school he met his first love, one Phœbe Hawkins, a very sweet, pretty girl, as he recalls her, and, of course, considerably his senior. How far he had advanced in the spelling of proper names at that period is shown by the well-authenticated fact that he put himself on record, once as "loving his love with an F, because she was Feeby!"

Poor Phœbe Hawkins died before she was out of her teens. The family moved to Poughkeepsie when The Boy was ten or twelve, and his mother and he went there one day from Red Hook, which was their summer home, to call upon his love. When they asked, at

the railroad-station, where the Hawkinses lived and how they could
find the house, they were told that the carriages for the funeral
would meet the next train. And, utterly unprepared for such a
greeting, for at latest accounts she had been in perfect health, they
stood, with her friends, by the side of Phœbe's open grave.

In his mind's eye The Boy, at the end of forty years, can see it all;
and his childish grief is still fresh in his memory. He had lost a bird
and a cat who were very dear to his heart, but death had never before seemed so real to him; never before had it come so near home.
He never played "funeral" again.

[p 16]
In 1851 or 1852 The Boy went to another dame's school. It was kept
by Miss Kilpatrick, on Franklin or North Moore Street. From this, as
he grew in years, he was sent to the Primary Department of the
North Moore Street Public School, at the corner of West Broadway,
where he remained three weeks, and where he contracted a whoop-
ing-cough which lasted him three months. The other boys used to
throw his hat upon an awning in the neighborhood, and then throw
their own hats up under the awning in order to bounce The Boy's
hat off—an amusement for which he never much cared. They were
not very nice boys, anyway, especially when they made fun of his
maternal grandfather, who was a trustee of the school, and who
sometimes noticed The Boy after the morning prayers were said.
The grandfather was very popular in the school. He came in every
day, stepped upon the raised platform at the principal's desk, and
said in his broad Scotch, "Good morning, boys!" to which the entire
body of pupils, at the top of their lungs, and with one voice, replied,
"*G-o-o-d morning, Mr. Scott!*" This was considered a great feature in
the school; and strangers used to come from all over the city to witness it. Somehow it made The Boy a little bit ashamed; he does not
know why. He would have liked it well enough, and been touched
by it, too, if it had been some other boy's grandfather. The Boy's
father [p 17]
was present once—The Boy's first day; but when he discovered that
the President of the Board of Trustees was going to call on him for a
speech he ran away; and The Boy would have given all his little
possessions to have run after him. The Boy knew then, as well as he
knows now, how his father felt; and he thinks of that occasion every

time he runs away from some after-dinner or occasional speech which he, himself, is called upon to make.

"GOOD MORNING, BOYS"

After his North Moore Street experiences The Boy was sent to study under men teachers in boys' schools; and he considered then that he was grown up.

The Boy, as has been said, was born without the sense of spell. The Rule of Three, it puzzled him, and fractions were as bad; and the proper placing of e and i, or i and e, the doubling of letters in the middle of words, and how to treat the addition of a suffix in "y" or "tion" "almost drove him mad," from his childhood up. He hated to go to school, but he loved to *play* school; and when Johnny Robertson and he were not conducting a pompous, public funeral—a certain oblong hat-brush, with a rosewood back, studded with brass tacks, serving as a coffin, in which lay the body of Henry Clay, Daniel Webster, or the Duke of Wellington, all of whom died when Johnny and The Boy were about eight years old—they were teaching each other the three [p 18]
immortal and exceedingly trying "R's"—reading, 'riting, and 'rithmetic—in a play-school. Their favorite spelling-book was a certain old cook-book, discarded by the head of the kitchen, and considered all that was necessary for their educational purpose. From this, one afternoon, Johnnie gave out "Dough-nut," with the following surprising result. Conscious of the puzzling presence of certain silent consonants and vowels, The Boy thus set it down: "D-O, dough, N-O-U-G-H-T, nut—doughnut!" and he went up head in a class of one, neither teacher nor pupil perceiving the marvellous transposition.

All The Boy's religious training was received at home, and almost his first text-book was "The Shorter Catechism," which, he confesses, he hated with all his little might. He had to learn and recite the answers to those awful questions as soon as he could recite at all, and, for years, without the slightest comprehension as to what it was all about. Even to this day he cannot tell just what "Effectual Calling," or "Justification," is; and I am sure that he shed more tears over "Effectual Calling" than would blot out the record of any number of infantile sins. He made up his youthful mind that if he could not be saved without "Effectual Calling"—whatever that was—he did not want to be saved at all. But he has thought better of it since.

PLAYING "SCHOOL"

It is proper to affirm here that The Boy did not [p 19]
acquire his occasional swear-words from "The Shorter Catechism."
They were born in him, as a fragment of Original Sin; and they
came out of him innocently and unwittingly, and only for purposes
of proper emphasis, long before the days of "Justification," and
even before he knew his A, B, C's.

His earliest visit to Scotland was made when he was but four or
five years of age, and long before he had assumed the dignity of
trousers, or had been sent to school. His father had gone to the old
home at St. Andrews hurriedly, upon the receipt of the news of the

serious illness of The Boy's grandmother, who died before they reached her. Naturally, The Boy has little recollection of that sad month of December, spent in his grandfather's house, except that it *was* sad. The weather was cold and wet; the house, even under ordinary circumstances, could not have been a very cheerful one for a youngster who had no companions of his own age. It looked out upon the German Ocean—which at that time of the year was always in a rage, or in the sulks—and it was called "Peep o' Day," because it received the very first rays of the sun as he rose upon the British Isles.

The Boy's chief amusement was the feeding of "flour-scones" and oat-cakes to an old goat, who lived in the neighborhood, and in daily walks with his grandfather, who seemed to find some little [p 20]
comfort and entertainment in the lad's childish prattle. He was then almost the only grandchild; and the old man was very proud of his manner and appearance, and particularly amused at certain gigantic efforts on The Boy's part to adapt his own short legs to the strides of his senior's long ones.

After they had interviewed the goat, and had watched the wrecks with which the wild shore was strewn, and had inspected the Castle in ruins, and the ruins of the Cathedral, The Boy would be shown his grandmother's new-made grave, and his own name in full—a common name in the family—upon the family tomb in the old kirkyard; all of which must have been very cheering to The Boy; although he could not read it for himself. And then, which was better, they would stand, hand in hand, for a long time in front of a certain candy-shop window, in which was displayed a little regiment of lead soldiers, marching in double file towards an imposing and impregnable tin fortress on the heights of barley-sugar. Of this spectacle they never tired; and they used to discuss how The Boy would arrange them if they belonged to him; with a sneaking hope on The Boy's part that, some day, they were to be his very own.

THE BOY'S SCOTCH GRANDFATHER

At the urgent request of the grandfather, the American contingent remained in St. Andrews until the end of the year; and The Boy still remembers vividly, and he will never forget, the dismal failure [p 21] of "Auld Lang Syne" as it was sung by the family, with clasped hands, as the clock struck and the New Year began. He sat up for the occasion—or, rather, was waked up for the occasion; and of all that family group he has been, for a decade or more, the only survivor. The mother of the house was but lately dead; the eldest son, and his son, were going, the next day, to the other side of the world; and every voice broke before the familiar verse came to an end.

As The Boy went off to his bed he was told that his grandfather had something for him, and he stood at his knee to receive—a Bible! That it was to be the lead soldiers and the tin citadel he never for a moment doubted; and the surprise and disappointment were very great. He seems to have had presence of mind enough to conceal his feelings, and to kiss and thank the dear old man for his gift. But as he climbed slowly up the stairs, in front of his mother, and with his Bible under his arm, she overheard him sob to himself, and murmur, in his great disgust: "Well, he has given me a book! And I wonder how in thunder he thinks I am going to read his damned Scotch!"

This display of precocious profanity and of innate patriotism, upon the part of a child who could not read at all, gave unqualified pleasure to the old gentleman, and he never tired of telling the story as long as he lived.

[p 22]
The Boy never saw the grandfather again. He had gone to the kirk-yard, to stay, before the next visit to St. Andrews was made; and now that kirk-yard holds everyone of The Boy's name and blood who is left in the town.
The Boy was taught, from the earliest awakening of his reasoning powers, that truth was to be told and to be respected, and that nothing was more wicked or more ungentlemanly than a broken promise. He learned very early to do as he was told, and not to do, under any consideration, what he had said he would not do. Upon this last point he was almost morbidly conscientious, although once, literally, he "beat about the bush." His aunt Margaret, always devoted to plants and to flowers, had, on the back stoop of his grandfather's house, a little grove of orange and lemon trees, in pots. Some of these were usually in fruit or in flower, and the fruit to The Boy was a great temptation. He was very fond of oranges, and it seemed to

him that a "home-made" orange, which he had never tasted, must be much better than a grocer's orange; as home-made cake was certainly preferable, even to the wonderful cakes made by the professional Mrs. Milderberger. He watched those little green oranges from day to day, as they gradually grew big and yellow in the sun. He promised faithfully that he would not pick any of them, but he had a notion that some of them might drop [p 23]
off. He never shook the trees, because he said he would not. But he shook the stoop! And he hung about the bush, which he was too honest to beat. One unusually tempting orange, which he had known from its bud-hood, finally overcame him. He did not pick it off, he did not shake it off; he compromised with his conscience by lying flat on his back and biting off a piece of it. It was not a very good action, nor was it a very good orange, and for that reason, perhaps, he went home immediately and told on himself. He told his mother. He did not tell his aunt Margaret. His mother did not seem to be as much shocked at his conduct as he was. But, in her own quiet way, she gave him to understand that promises were not made to be cracked any more than they were made to be broken — that he had been false to himself in heart, if not in deed, and that he must go back and make it "all right" with his aunt Margaret. She did not seem to be very much shocked, either; he could not tell why. But they punished The Boy. They made him eat the rest of the orange!

THE HOUSE OF THE BOY'S GRANDFATHER — CORNER OF HUDSON AND NORTH MOORE STREETS

He lost all subsequent interest in that tropical glade, and he has never cared much for domestic oranges since.

Among the many bumps which are still conspicuously absent in The Boy's phrenological development are the bumps of Music and Locality. He [p 24]
whistled as soon as he acquired front teeth; and he has been singing "God Save the Queen" at the St. Andrew's Society dinners, on November the 30th, ever since he came of age. But that is as far as his sense of harmony goes. He took music-lessons for three quarters, and then his mother gave it up in despair. The instrument was a piano. The Boy could not stretch an octave with his right hand, the little finger of which had been broken by a shinny-stick; and he could not do anything whatever with his left hand. He was constantly dropping his bass-notes, which, he said, were "understood." And even Miss Ferguson — most patient of teachers — declared that it was of no use.

The piano to The Boy has been the most offensive of instruments ever since. And when his mother's old piano, graceful in form, and with curved legs which are still greatly admired, lost its tone, and was transformed into a sideboard, he felt, for the first time, that music had charms.

He had to practise half an hour a day, by a thirty-minute sand-glass that could *not* be set ahead; and he shed tears enough over "The Carnival of Venice" to have raised the tide in the Grand Canal. They blurred the sharps and the flats on the music-books — those tears; they ran the crotchets and the quavers together, and, rolling down his cheeks, they even splashed upon his not very clean little [p 25] hands; and, literally, they covered the keys with mud.

"ALWAYS IN THE WAY"

Another serious trial to The Boy was dancing-school. In the first place, he could not turn round without becoming dizzy; in the second place, he could not learn the steps to turn round with; and in the third place, when he did dance he had to dance with a girl! There was not a boy in all Charraud's, or in all Dodworth's, who could escort a girl back to her seat, after the dance was over, in better time, or make his "thank-you bow" with less delay. His only voluntary terpsichorean effort at a party was the march to supper; and the only steps he ever took with anything like success were during the promenade in the lancers. In "hands-all-round" he invariably started with the wrong hand; and if in the set there were girls big enough to wear long dresses, he never failed to tear such out at the gathers. If anybody fell down in the polka it was always The Boy; and if anybody bumped into anybody else, The Boy was always the bumper, unless his partner could hold him up and steer him straight.

Games, at parties, he enjoyed more than dancing, although he did not care very much for "Pillows and Keys," until he became courageous enough to kneel before somebody except his maiden aunts. "Porter" was less embarrassing, because, when the door was shut, nobody but the little girl who called [p 26]
him but could tell whether he kissed her or not. All this happened a long time ago!

The only social function in which The Boy took any interest whatever was the making of New-Year's calls. Not that he cared to make New-Year's calls in themselves, but because he wanted to make more New-Year's calls than were made by any other boy. His "list," based upon last year's list, was commenced about February 1; and it contained the names of every person whom The Boy knew, or thought he knew, whether that person knew The Boy or not, from Mrs. Penrice, who boarded opposite the Bowling Green, to the Leggats and the Faures, who lived near Washington Parade Ground, the extreme social limits of his city in those days. He usually began by making a formal call upon his own mother, who allowed him to taste the pickled oysters as early as ten in the morning; and he invariably wound up by calling upon Ann Hughes in the kitchen, where he met the soap-fat man, who was above his profession, and likewise the sexton of Ann Hughes's church, who generally came with Billy, the barber on the corner of Franklin Street. There were certain calls The Boy always made with his father, during which he did not partake of pickled oysters; but he had pickled oysters everywhere else; and they never seemed to do him any serious harm.

READY FOR A NEW-YEAR'S CALL

[p 27]

The Boy, if possible, kept his new overcoat until New Year's Day—
and he never left it in the hall when he called! He always wore new
green kid gloves—why green?—fastened at the wrists with a single
hook and eye; and he never took off his kid gloves when he called,
except on that particular New Year's Day when his aunt Charlotte
gave him the bloodstone seal-ring, which, at first, was too big for his
little finger,—the only finger on which a seal-ring *could* be worn—
and had to be made temporarily smaller with a piece of string.

When he received, the next New Year, new studs and a scarf-
pin—all bloodstones, to match the ring—he exhibited no little inge-
nuity of toilet in displaying them both, because studs are hardly
visible when one wears a scarf, unless the scarf is kept out of the
perpendicular by stuffing one end of it into the sleeve of a jacket;

36

which requires constant attention and a good deal of bodily contortion.

When The Boy met Johnny Robertson or Joe Stuart making calls, they never recognized each other, except when they were calling together, which did not often occur. It was an important rule in their social code to appear as strangers in-doors, although they would wait for each other outside, and compare lists. When they *did* present themselves collectively in any drawing-room, one boy — usually The Boy's cousin Lew — was detailed to whisper "T. [p 28] T." when he considered that the proper limit of the call was reached. "T. T." stood for "Time to Travel"; and at the signal all conversation was abruptly interrupted, and the party trooped out in single file. The idea was not original with the boys. It was borrowed from the hook-and-ladder company, which made all *its* calls in a body, and in two of Kipp and Brown's stages, hired for the entire day. The boys always walked.

The great drawbacks to the custom of making New-Year's calls were the calls which *had* to be made after the day's hard work was supposed to be over, and when The Boy and his father, returning home very tired, were told that they *must* call upon Mrs. Somebody, and upon Mrs. Somebody-else, whom they had neglected to visit, because the husbands and the sons of these ladies had called upon the mother of The Boy. New Year's Day was not the shortest day of the year, by any means, but it was absolutely necessary to return the Somebody's call, no matter how late the hour, or how tired the victims of the social law. And it bored the ladies of the Somebody household as much as it bored the father and The Boy.

A NEW-YEAR'S CALL

The Boy was always getting lost. The very first time he went out alone he got lost! Told not to go off the block, he walked as far as the corner of Leonard Street, put his arm around the lamp-post, [p 29]

swung himself in a circle, had his head turned the wrong way, and marched off, at a right angle, along the side street, with no home visible anywhere, and not a familiar sign in sight. A ship at sea without a rudder, a solitary wanderer in the Great American Desert without a compass, could not have been more utterly astray. The Boy was so demoralized that he forgot his name and address; and when a kindly policeman picked him up, and carried him over the way, to the Leonard Street station-house for identification, he felt as if the end of everything had come. It was bad enough to be arrested, but how was he to satisfy his own conscience, and explain matters to his mother, when it was discovered that he had broken his solemn promise, and crossed the street? He had no pocket-handkerchief; and he remembers that he spoiled the long silk streamers of his Glengarry bonnet by wiping his eyes upon them. He was recognized by his Forty-second-plaid gingham frock, a familiar object in the neighborhood, and he was carried back to his parents, who had not had time to miss him, and who, consequently, were not distracted. He lost nothing by the adventure but himself, his self-respect, a pint of tears — and one shoe.

He was afterwards lost in Greenwich Street, having gone there on the back step of an ice-cart; and once he was conveyed as far as the Hudson River Railroad Depot, at Chambers Street, on his sled, which he had [p 30]
hitched to the milkman's wagon, and could not untie. This was very serious, indeed; for The Boy realized that he had not only lost himself but his sleigh, too. Aunt Henrietta found The Boy sitting disconsolately in front of Wall's bake-shop; but the sleigh did not turn up for several days. It was finally discovered, badly scratched, in the possession of "The Head of the Rovers."

"The Hounds" and "The Rovers" were rival bands of boys, not in The Boy's set, who for many years made out-door life miserable to The Boy and to his friends. They threw stones and mud at each other, and at everybody else; and The Boy was not infrequently blamed for the windows they broke. They punched all the little boys who were better dressed than they were, and they were even depraved enough, and mean enough, to tell the driver every time The Boy or Johnny Robertson attempted to "cut behind."

TOM RILEY'S LIBERTY POLE

There was also a band of unattached guerillas who aspired to be, and often pretended to be, either "Hounds" or "Rovers"—they did not care which. They always hunted in couples, and if they met The Boy alone they asked him to which of the organizations he himself belonged. If he said he was a "Rover," they claimed to be "Hounds," and pounded him. If he declared himself in sympathy with the "Hounds," they hoisted the "Rovers'" colors, and [p 31] punched him again. If he disclaimed both associations, they punched him anyway, on general principles. "The Head of the Rovers" was subsequently killed, in front of Tom Riley's liberty-pole in

40

Franklin Street, in a fireman's riot, and "The Chief of the Hounds," who had a club-foot, became a respectable egg-merchant, with a stand in Washington Market, near the Root-beer Woman's place of business, on the south side. The Boy met two of the gang near the Desbrosses Street Ferry only the other day; but they did not recognize The Boy.

The only spot where The Boy felt really safe from the interference of "The Hounds" and "The Rovers" was in St. John's Square, that delightful oasis in the desert of brick and mortar and cobble-stones which was known as the Fifth Ward. It was a private enclosure, bounded on the north by Laight Street, on the south by Beach Street, on the east by Varick Street, and on the west by Hudson Street; and its site is now occupied by the great freight-warehouses of the New York Central and Hudson River Railroad Company.

In the "Fifties," and long before, it was a private park, to which only the property owners in its immediate neighborhood had access. It possessed fine old trees, winding gravel-walks, and meadows of grass. In the centre was a fountain, whereupon, in the proper season, the children were allowed to skate on both [p 32] feet, which was a great improvement over the one-foot gutter-slides outside. The Park was surrounded by a high iron railing, broken here and there by massive gates, to which The Boy had a key. But he always climbed over. It was a point of etiquette, in The Boy's set, to climb over on all occasions, whether the gates were unlocked or not. And The Boy, many a time, has been known to climb over a gate, although it stood wide open! He not infrequently tore his clothes on the sharp spikes by which the gates were surmounted; but that made no difference to The Boy—until he went home!

The Boy once had a fight in the Park, with Bill Rice, about a certain lignum-vitæ peg-top, of which The Boy was very fond, and which Bill Rice kicked into the fountain. The Boy got mad, which was wrong and foolish of The Boy; and The Boy, also, got licked. And The Boy never could make his mother understand why he was silly and careless enough to cut his under-lip by knocking it against Bill Rice's knuckles. Bill subsequently apologized by saying that he did not mean to kick the top into the fountain. He merely meant to kick the top. And it was all made up.

THE BOY ALWAYS CLIMBED OVER

The Boy did not fight much. His nose was too long. It seemed that he could not reach the end of it with his fists when he fought; and that the other fellows could always reach it with theirs, no matter [p 33]

42

how far out, or how scientifically, his left arm was extended. It was "One, two, three—and recover"—on The Boy's nose! The Boy was a good runner. His legs were the only part of his anatomy which seemed to him as long as his nose. And his legs saved his nose in many a fierce encounter.

The Boy first had daily admission to St. John's Park after the family moved to Hubert Street, when The Boy was about ten years old; and for half a decade or more it was his happy hunting-ground—when he was not kept in school! It was a particularly pleasant place in the autumn and winter months; for he could then gather "smoking-beans" and horse-chestnuts; and he could roam at will all over the grounds without any hateful warning to "Keep Off the Grass."

The old gardener, generally a savage defender of the place, who had no sense of humor as it was exhibited in boy nature, sometimes let the boys rake the dead leaves into great heaps and make bonfires of them, if the wind happened to be in the right direction. And then what larks! The bonfire was a house on fire, and the great garden-roller, a very heavy affair, was "Engine No. 42," with which the boys ran to put the fire out. They all shouted as loudly and as unnecessarily as real firemen did, in those days; the foreman gave his orders through a real trumpet, and one boy had a real fireman's hat
[p 34]
with "Engine No. 42" on it. He was chief engineer, but he did not run with the machine: not because he was chief engineer, but because while in active motion he could not keep his hat on. It was his father's hat, and its extraordinary weight was considerably increased by the wads of newspaper packed in the lining to make it fit. The chief engineer held the position for life on the strength of the hat, which he would not lend to anybody else. The rest of the officers of the company were elected, *viva voce*, every time there was a fire.

This entertainment came to an end, like everything else, when the gardener chained the roller to the tool-house, after Bob Stuart fell under the machine and was rolled so flat that he had to be carried home on a stretcher, made of overcoats tied together by the sleeves. That is the only recorded instance in which the boys, particularly Bob, left the Park without climbing over. And the bells sounded a "general alarm." The dent made in the path by Bob's body was on exhibition until the next snow-storm.

THE CHIEF ENGINEER
The favorite amusements in the Park were shinny, baseball, one-old-cat, and fires. The Columbia Baseball Club was organized in 1853 or 1854. It had nine members, and The Boy was secretary and treasurer. The uniform consisted chiefly of a black leather belt with the initials

C B B C

in white

letters, hand-painted, and generally turned the wrong way. [p 35]
The first base was an ailantus-tree; the second base was another
ailantus-tree; the third base was a button-ball-tree; the home base
was a marble head-stone, brought for that purpose from an old
burying-ground not far away; and "over the fence" was a home-
run. A player was caught out on the second bounce, and he was
"out" if hit by a ball thrown at him as he ran. The Boy was put out
once by a crack on the ear, which put The Boy out very much.

"The Hounds" and "The Rovers" challenged "The Columbias"
repeatedly. But that was looked upon simply as an excuse to get
into the Park, and the challenges were never accepted. The chal-
lengers were forced to content themselves with running off with the
balls which went over the fence; an action on their part which made
home-runs through that medium very unpopular and very expen-
sive. In the whole history of "The Hounds" and "The Rovers," nothing that they pirated was ever returned but The Boy's sled.

Contemporary with the Columbia Baseball Club was a so-called
"Mind-cultivating Society," organized by the undergraduates of
McElligott's School, in Greene Street. The Boy, as usual, was secretary when he was not treasurer. The object was "Debates," but all
the debating was done at the business meetings, and no mind ever
became sufficiently [p 36]
cultivated to master the intricacies of parliamentary law. The members called it a Secret Society, and on their jackets they wore, as
conspicuously as possible, a badge-pin consisting of a blue enam-
elled circlet containing Greek letters in gold. In a very short time the
badge-pin was all that was left of the Society; but to this day the
secret of the Society has never been disclosed. No one ever knew, or
will ever know, what the Greek letters stood for—not even the
members themselves.
The Boy was never a regular member of any fire-company, but almost as long as the old Volunteer Fire Department existed, he was
what was known as a "Runner." He was attached, in a sort of brevet
way, to "Pearl Hose No. 28," and, later, to "11 Hook and Ladder."
He knew all the fire districts into which the city was then divided;
his ear was always alert, even in the St. John's Park days, for the
sound of the alarm-bell, and he ran to every fire at any hour of the
day or night, up to ten o'clock P.M. He did not do much when he

got to the fire but stand around and "holler." But once—a proud moment—he helped steer the hook-and-ladder truck to a false alarm in Macdougal Street—and once—a very proud moment, indeed—he went into a tenement-house, near Dr. Thompson's church, in Grand Street, and carried two negro babies down-stairs in his arms. There was no earthly reason why the [p 37]
babies should not have been left in their beds; and the colored family did not like it, because the babies caught cold! But The Boy, for once in his life, tasted the delights of self-conscious heroism.

"MRS. ROBERTSON DESCENDED IN FORCE UPON THE DE-
VOTED BAND"

When The Boy, as a bigger boy, was not running to fires he was
going to theatres, the greater part of his allowance being spent in
the box-offices of Burton's Chambers Street house, of Brougham's

Lyceum, corner of Broome Street and Broadway, of Niblo's, and of Castle Garden. There were no afternoon performances in those days, except now and then when the Ravels were at Castle Garden; and the admission to pit and galleries was usually two shillings — otherwise, twenty-five cents. His first play, so far as he remembers, was "The Stranger," a play dismal enough to destroy any taste for the drama, one would suppose, in any juvenile mind. He never cared very much to see "The Stranger" again, but nothing that was a play was too deep or too heavy for him. He never saw the end of any of the more elaborate productions, unless his father took him to the theatre (as once in a while he did), for it was a strict rule of the house, until The Boy was well up in his teens, that he must be in by ten o'clock. His father did not ask him where he was going, or where he had been; but the curfew in Hubert Street tolled at ten. The Boy calculated carefully and exactly how many minutes it took him to [p 38]
run to Hubert Street from Brougham's or from Burton's; and by the middle of the second act his watch — a small silver affair with a hunting-case, in which he could not keep an uncracked crystal — was always in his hand. He never disobeyed his father, and for years he never knew what became of Claude Melnotte after he went to the wars; or if Damon got back in time to save Pythias before the curtain fell. The Boy, naturally, had a most meagre notion as to what all these plays were about, but he enjoyed his fragments of them as he rarely enjoys plays now. Sometimes, in these days, when the air is bad, and plays are worse, and big hats are worse than either, he wishes that he were forced to leave the modern play-house at nine-forty-five, on pain of no supper that night, or twenty lines of "Virgil" the next day.

THE BOY AS VIRGINIUS

On very stormy afternoons the boys played theatre in the large garret of The Boy's Hubert Street house; a convenient closet, with a door and a window, serving for the Castle of Elsinore in "Hamlet," for the gunroom of the ship in "Black-eyed Susan," or for the studio of Phidias in "The Marble Heart," as the case might be. "The Brazilian Ape," as requiring more action than words, was a favorite entertainment, only they all wanted to play Jocko the Ape; and they would have made no little success out of the "Lady of Lyons" if any of them had [p 39]

been willing to play Pauline. Their costumes and properties were slight and not always accurate, but they could "launch the curse of Rome," and describe "two hearts beating as one," in a manner rarely equalled on the regular stage. The only thing they really lacked was an audience, neither Lizzie Gustin nor Ann Hughes ever being able to sit through more than one act at a time. When The Boy, as Virginius, with his uncle Aleck's sword-cane, stabbed all the feathers out of the pillow which represented the martyred Virginia; and when Joe Stuart, as Falstaff, broke the bottom out of Ann Hughes's clothes-basket, the license was revoked, and the season came to an untimely end.

Until the beginning of the weekly, or the fortnightly, sailings of the Collins line of steamers from the foot of Canal Street (a spectacle which they never missed in any weather), Joe Stuart, Johnny Robertson, and The Boy played "The Deerslayer" every Saturday in the back-yard of The Boy's house. The area-way was Glimmer-glass, in which they fished, and on which they canoed; the back-stoop was Muskrat Castle; the rabbits were all the wild beasts of the Forest; Johnny was Hawk-Eye, The Boy was Hurry Harry, and Joe Stuart was Chingachgook. Their only food was half-baked potatoes— sweet potatoes if possible—which they cooked themselves and ate ravenously, with butter and salt, if Ann Hughes was [p 40] amiable, and entirely unseasoned if Ann was disposed to be disobliging.

They talked what they fondly believed was the dialect of the Delaware tribe, and they were constantly on the lookout for the approaches of Rivenoak, or the Panther, who were represented by any member of the family who chanced to stray into the enclosure. They carefully turned their toes in when they walked, making so much effort in this matter that it took a great deal of dancing-school to get their feet back to the "first position" again; and they even painted their faces when they were on the war-path. The rabbits had the worst of it!

The campaign came to a sudden and disastrous conclusion when the hostile tribes, headed by Mrs. Robertson, descended in force upon the devoted band, because Chingachgook broke one of Hawk-Eye's front teeth with an arrow, aimed at the biggest of the rabbits,

which was crouching by the side of the roots of the grape-vine, and
playing that he was a panther of enormous size.

JOHNNY ROBERTSON
Johnny Robertson and The Boy had one great superstition—to wit,
Cracks! For some now inexplicable reason they thought it unlucky
to step on cracks; and they made daily and hourly spectacles of
themselves in the streets by the eccentric irregularity of their gait.
Now they would take long strides, like a pair of ostriches, and now
short, quick [p 41]
steps, like a couple of robins; now they would hop on both feet, like
a brace of sparrows; now they would walk on their heels, now on
their toes; now with their toes turned in, now with their toes turned
out—at right angles, in a splay-footed way; now they would walk
with their feet crossed, after the manner of the hands of very fancy,
old-fashioned piano-players, skipping from base to treble—over
cracks. The whole performance would have driven a sensitive drill-
sergeant or ballet-master to distraction. And when they came to a
brick sidewalk they would go all around the block to avoid it. They
could cross Hudson Street on the cobblestones with great effort, and

in great danger of being run over; but they could not possibly travel upon a brick pavement, and avoid the cracks. What would have happened to them if they *did* step on a crack they did not exactly know. But, for all that, they never stepped on cracks—of their own free will!

The Boy's earliest attempts at versification were found, the other day, in an old desk, and at the end of almost half a century. The copy is in his own boyish, ill-spelled print; and it bears no date. The present owner, his aunt Henrietta, well remembers the circumstances and the occasion, however, having been an active participant in the acts the poem describes, although she avers that she had no hand in its composition. The original, it seems, was [p 42] transcribed by The Boy upon the cover of a soap-box, which served as a head-stone to one of the graves in his family burying-ground, situated in the back-yard of the Hudson Street house, from which he was taken before he was nine years of age. The monument stood against the fence, and this is the legend it bore—rhyme, rhythm, metre, and orthography being carefully preserved:

> "Three little kitens of our old cat
> Were berrid this day in this grassplat.
> They came to there deth in an old slop pale,
> And after loosing their breth
> They were pulled out by the tale.
> These three little kitens have returned to their
> maker,
> And were put in the grave by The Boy,
> Undertaker."

At about this period The Boy officiated at the funeral of another cat, but in a somewhat more exalted capacity. It was the Cranes' cat, at Red Hook—a Maltese lady, who always had yellow kittens. The Boy does not remember the cause of the cat's death, but he thinks that Uncle Andrew Knox ran over her, with the "dyspepsia-wagon"—so called because it had no springs. Anyway, the cat died, [p 43] and had to be buried. The grave was dug in the garden of the tavern, near the swinging-gate to the stable, and the whole family attended the services. Jane Purdy, in a deep crape veil, was the chief mourner; The Boy's aunts were pall-bearers, in white scarves; The

Boy was the clergyman; while the kittens—who did not look at all like their mother—were on hand in a funeral basket, with black shoestrings tied around their necks.

JANE PURDY

Jane was supposed to be the disconsolate widow. She certainly looked the part to perfection; and it never occurred to any of them that a cat, with kittens, could not possibly have left a widow behind her.

The ceremony was most impressive; the bereaved kittens were loud in their grief; when, suddenly, the village-bell tolled for the death of an old gentleman whom everybody loved, and the comedy became a tragedy. The older children were conscience-stricken at the mummery, and they ran, demoralized and shocked, into the house, leaving The Boy and the kittens behind them. Jane Purdy tripped over her veil, and one of the kittens was stepped on in the crush. But The Boy proceeded with the funeral.

When The Boy got as far as a room of his own, papered with scenes from circus-posters, and peopled by tin soldiers, he used to play that his bed was the barge *Mayflower*, running from Barrytown to the [p 44]
foot of Jay Street, North River, and that he was her captain and crew. She made nightly trips between the two ports; and by day, when she was not tied up to the door-knob—which was Barrytown—she was moored to the handle of the wash-stand drawer— which was the dock at New York. She never was wrecked, and she never ran aground; but great was the excitement of The Boy when, as not infrequently was the case, on occasions of sweeping, Hannah, the up-stairs girl, set her adrift.

The *Mayflower* was seriously damaged by fire once, owing to the careless use, by a deck-hand, of a piece of punk on the night before the Fourth of July; this same deck-hand being nearly blown up early the very next morning by a bunch of fire-crackers which went off— by themselves—in his lap. He did not know, for a second or two, whether the barge had burst her boiler or had been struck by lightning!

JOE STUART

Barrytown is the river port of Red Hook—a charming Dutchess County hamlet in which The Boy spent the first summer of his life, and in which he spent the better part of every succeeding summer for a quarter of a century; and he sometimes goes there yet, although many of the names he knows were carved, in the long-agoes, on the tomb. He always went up and down, in those days, on the *Mayflower*, the real boat of that name, which was hardly more [p 45] real to him than was the trundle-bed of his vivid, nightly imagination. They sailed from New York at five o'clock P.M., an hour looked for, and longed for, by The Boy, as the very beginning of summer, with all its delightful young charms; and they arrived at their destination about five of the clock the next morning, by which time The Boy was wide awake, and on the lookout for Lasher's Stage, in which he was to travel the intervening three miles. And eagerly he recognized, and loved, every landmark on the road. Barringer's Corner; the half-way tree; the road to the creek and to Madame Knox's; and, at last, the village itself, and the tavern, and the tobacco-factory, and Massoneau's store, over the way; and then, when Jane Purdy had shown him the new kittens and the little chickens, and he had talked to "Fido" and "Fanny," or to Fido alone after Fanny was stolen by gypsies — Fanny was Fido's wife, and a poodle — he rushed off to see Bob Hendricks, who was just his own age, barring a week, and who has been his warm friend for more than half a century; and then what good times The Boy had! Bob was possessed of a grandfather who could make kites, and swings, and parallel-bars, and things which The Boy liked; and Bob had a mother — and he has her yet, happy Bob! — who made the most wonderful of cookies, perfectly round, with sparkling [p 46] globules of sugar on them, and little round holes in the middle; and Bob and The Boy for days, and weeks, and months together hen's-egged, and rode in the hay-carts, and went for the mail every noon, and boosted each other up into the best pound-sweet-tree in the neighborhood; and pelted each other with little green apples, which weighed about a pound to the peck; and gathered currants and chestnuts in season; and with long straws they sucked new cider out of bung-holes; and learned to swim; and caught their first fish; and did all the pleasant things that all boys do.

At Red Hook they smoked their first cigar — half a cigar, left by uncle Phil — and they wished they hadn't! And at Red Hook they disobeyed their mothers once, and were found out. They were told not to go wading in the creek upon pain of not going to the creek at all; and for weeks they were deprived of the delights of the society of the Faure boys, through whose domain the creek ran, because, when they went to bed on that disastrous night, it was discovered that Bob had on The Boy's stockings, and that The Boy was wearing Bob's socks; a piece of circumstantial evidence which convicted them both. When the embargo was raised and they next went to the creek, it is remembered that Bob tore his trousers in climbing over a log, and that The Boy fell in altogether.

BOB HENDRICKS
[p 47]
The Boy usually kept his promises, however, and he was known
even to keep a candy-cane — twenty-eight inches long, red and
white striped like a barber's pole — for a fortnight, because his
mother limited him to the consumption of two inches a day. But he
could not keep any knees to his trousers; and when The Boy's
mother threatened to sew buttons — brass buttons, with sharp and
penetrating eyes — on to that particular portion of the garment in
question, he wanted to know, in all innocence, how they expected
him to say his prayers!

One of Bob's earliest recollections of The Boy is connected with a
toy express-wagon on four wheels, which could almost turn around
on its own axis. The Boy imported this vehicle into Red Hook one
summer, and they used it for the transportation of their chestnuts
and their currants and their apples, green and ripe, and the mail,
and most of the dust of the road; and Bob thinks, to this day, that

nothing in all these after years has given him so much profound satisfaction and enjoyment as did that little cart.

Bob remembers, too — what The Boy tries to forget — The Boy's daily practice of half an hour on the piano borrowed by The Boy's mother from Mrs. Bates for that dire purpose. Mrs. Bates's piano is almost the only unpleasant thing associated with Red Hook in all The Boy's experience of that happy village. It was pretty hard on The Boy, because, in [p 48]
The Boy's mind, Red Hook should have been a place of unbroken delights. But The Boy's mother wanted to make an all-round man of him, and when his mother said so, of course it had to be done or tried. Bob used to go with The Boy as far as Dr. Bates's house, and then hang about on the gate until The Boy was released; and he asserts that the music which came out of the window in response to The Boy's inharmonic touch had no power whatever to soothe his own savage young breast. He attributes all his later disinclination to music to those dreary thirty minutes of impatient waiting.

The piano and its effect upon The Boy's uncertain temper *may* have been the innocent cause of the first, and only, approach to a quarrel which The Boy and Bob ever had. The prime cause, however, was, of course, a girl! They were playing, that afternoon, at Cholwell Knox's, when Cholwell said something about Julia Booth which Bob resented, and there was a fight, The Boy taking Cholwell's part; why, he cannot say, unless it was because of his jealousy of Bob's affection and admiration for that charming young teacher, who won all hearts in the village, The Boy's among the number. Anyway, Bob was driven from the field by the hard little green apples of the Knox orchard; more hurt, he declares, by the desertion of his ally than by all the blows he received.

MUSIC LESSONS
[p 49]
It never happened again, dear Bob, and, please God, it never will!

Another trouble The Boy had in Red Hook was Dr. McNamee, a resident dentist, who operated upon The Boy, now and then. He was a little more gentle than was The Boy's city dentist, Dr. Castle; but he hurt, for all that. Dr. Castle lived in Fourth Street, opposite Washington Parade Ground, and on the same block with Clarke and Fanning's school. And to this day The Boy would go miles out of his way rather than pass Dr. Castle's house. Personally Dr. Castle was a delightful man, who told The Boy amusing stories, which The Boy could not laugh at while his mouth was wide open. But professionally Dr. Castle was to The Boy an awful horror, of whom he always dreamed when his dreams were particularly bad. As he looks back upon his boyhood, with its frequent toothache and its long hours in the dentists' chairs, The Boy sometimes thinks that if he had his life to live over again, and could not go through it without teeth, he would prefer not to be born at all!

It has rather amused The Boy, in his middle age, to learn of the impressions he made upon Red Hook in his extreme youth. Bob, as has been shown, associates him with a little cart, and with a good deal of the concord of sweet sounds. One old friend remembers nothing but his phenomenal capacity for [p 50]
the consumption of chicken pot-pie. Another old friend can recall the scrupulously clean white duck suits which he wore of afternoons, and also the blue-checked long apron which he was forced to wear in the mornings; both of them exceedingly distasteful to The Boy, because the apron was a girl's garment, and because the duck suit meant "dress-up," and only the mildest of genteel play; while Bob's sister dwells chiefly now upon the wonderful valentine The Boy sent once to Zillah Crane. It was so large that it had to have an especial envelope made to fit it; and it was so magnificent, and so delicate, that, notwithstanding the envelope, it came in a box of its own. It had actual lace, and pinkish Cupids reclining on light-blue clouds; and in the centre of all was a compressible bird-cage, which, when it was pulled out, like an accordion, displayed not a dove merely, but a plain gold ring — a real ring, made of real gold. Nothing like it had ever been seen before in all Dutchess County; and it was seen and envied by every girl of Zillah's age between Rhinebeck and Tivoli, between Barrytown and Pine Plains.

The Boy did an extensive business in the valentine line, in the days when February Fourteenth meant much more to boys than it does now. He sent sentimental valentines to Phœbe Hawkins and comic valentines to Ann Hughes, both of them written anonymously, and both directed in a disguised hand. [p 51]
But both recipients always knew from whom they came; and, in all probability, neither of them was much affected by the receipt. The Boy, as he has put on record elsewhere, never really, in his inmost heart, thought that comic valentines were so very comic, because those that came to him usually reflected upon his nose, or were illuminated with portraits of gentlemen of all ages adorned with supernaturally red hair.

In later years, when Bob and The Boy could swim—a little—and had learned to take care of themselves in water over their heads, the mill-pond at Red Hook played an important part in their daily life there. They sailed it, and fished it, and camped out on its banks, with Ed Curtis—before Ed went to West Point—and with Dick Hawley, Josie Briggs, and Frank Rodgers, all first-rate fellows. But that is another story.

The Boy was asked, a year or two ago, to write a paper upon "The Books of his Boyhood." And when he came to think the matter over he discovered, to his surprise, that the Books of his Boyhood consisted of but one book! It was bound in two twelvemo green cloth volumes; it bore the date of 1850, and it was filled with pictorial illustrations of "The Personal History and Experiences of David Copperfield, the Younger." It was the first book The Boy ever read, and he thought then, and [p 52]
sometimes he thinks now, that it was the greatest book ever written. The traditional books of the childhood of other children came later to The Boy: "Robinson Crusoe," and the celebrated "Swiss Family" of the same name; "The Desert Home," of Mayne Reid; Marryat's "Peter Simple"; "The Leather Stocking Tales"; "Rob Roy"; and "The Three Guardsmen" were well thumbed and well liked; but they were not The Boy's first love in fiction, and they never usurped, in his affections, the place of the true account of David Copperfield. It was a queer book to have absorbed the time and attention of a boy of eight or nine, who had to skip the big words, who did not under-stand it all, but who cried, as he has cried but once since, whenever

he came to that dreadful chapter which tells the story of the taking away of David's mother, and of David's utter, hopeless desolation over his loss.

How the book came into The Boy's possession he cannot now remember, nor is he sure that his parents realized how much, or how often, he was engrossed in its contents. It cheered him in the measles, it comforted him in the mumps. He took it to school with him, and he took it to bed with him; and he read it, over and over again, especially the early chapters; for he did not care so much for David after David became Trotwood, and fell in love.

When, in 1852, after his grandfather's death, The [p 53] Boy first saw London, it was not the London of the Romans, the Saxons, or the Normans, or the London of the Plantagenets or the Tudors, but the London of the Micawbers and the Traddleses, the London of Murdstone and Grinby, the London of Dora's Aunt and of Jip. On his arrival at Euston Station the first object upon which his eyes fell was a donkey-cart, a large wooden tray on wheels, driven, at a rapid pace, by a long-legged young man, and followed, at a pace hardly so rapid, by a boy of about his own age, who seemed in great mental distress. This was the opening scene. And London, from that moment, became to him, and still remains, a great moving panorama of David Copperfield.
He saw the Orfling, that first evening, snorting along Tottenham Court Road; he saw Mealy Potatoes, in a ragged apron and a paper cap, lounging along Broad Street; he saw Martha disappear swiftly and silently into one of the dirty streets leading from Seven Dials; he saw innumerable public-houses — the Lion, or the Lion and something else — in anyone of which David might have consumed that memorable glass of Genuine Stunning ale with a good head on it. As they drove through St. Martin's Lane, and past a court at the back of the church, he even got a glimpse of the exterior of the shop where was sold a special pudding, made of currants, but dear; a two-pennyworth being no larger than a pennyworth of [p 54] more ordinary pudding at any other establishment in the neighborhood. And, to crown all, when he looked out of his back bedroom window, at Morley's Hotel, he discovered that he was looking at the actual bedroom windows of the Golden Cross on the Strand, in which Steerforth and little Copperfield had that disastrous meeting

which indirectly brought so much sorrow to so many innocent men
and women.

This was but the beginning of countless similar experiences, and the
beginning of a love for Landmarks of a more important but hardly
of a more delightful character. Hungerford Market and Hungerford
Stairs, with the blacking-warehouse abutting on the water when the
tide was in, and on the mud when the tide was out, still stood near
Morley's in 1852; and very close to them stood then, and still stands
to-day, the old house in Buckingham Street, Adelphi, where, with
Mrs. Crupp, Trotwood Copperfield found his lodgings when he
began his new life with Spenlow and Jorkins. These chambers, once
the home of Clarkson Stanfield, and since of Mr. William Black and
of Dr. B. E. Martin, became, in later days, very familiar to The Boy,
and still are haunted by the great crowd of the ghosts of the past.
The Boy has seen there, within a few years, and with his eyes wide
open, the spirits of Traddles, of Micawber, of Steerforth, of Mr.
Dick, of Clara [p 55]
Peggotty and Daniel, of Uriah Heep — the last slept one evening on
the sofa pillows before the fire, you may remember — and of Aunt
Betsy herself. But in 1852 he could only look at the outside of the
house, and, now and then, when the door was open, get a glimpse
of the stairs down which some one fell and rolled, one evening,
when somebody else said it was Copperfield!

The Boy never walked along the streets of London by his father's
side during that memorable summer without meeting, in fancy,
some friend of David's, without passing some spot that David
knew, and loved, or hated. And he recognized St. Paul's Cathedral
at the first glance, because it had figured as an illustration on the
cover of Peggotty's work-box!

Perhaps the event which gave him the greatest pleasure was a casu-
al meeting with little Miss Moucher in a green omnibus coming
from the top of Baker Street to Trafalgar Square. It could not possibly have been anybody else. There were the same large head and
face, the same short arms. "Throat she had none; waist she had
none; legs she had none, worth mentioning." The Boy can still hear
the pattering of the rain on the rattly windows of that lumbering
green omnibus; he can remember every detail of the impressive
drive; and Miss Moucher, and the fact of her existence in the flesh,

and there present, [p 56]
wiped from his mind every trace of Mme. Tussaud's famous gallery, and the waxworks it contained.

This was the Book of The Boy's Boyhood. He does not recommend it as the exclusive literature of their boyhood to other boys; but out of it The Boy knows that he got nothing but what was healthful and helping. It taught him to abominate selfish brutality and sneaking falsehood, as they were exhibited in the Murdstones and the Heeps; it taught him to keep Charles I., and other fads, out of his "Memorials"; it taught him to avoid rash expenditure as it was practised by the Micawbers; it showed him that a man like Steerforth might be the best of good fellows and at the same time the worst and most dangerous of companions; it showed, on the other hand, that true friends like Traddles are worth having and worth keeping; it introduced him to the devoted, sisterly affection of a woman like Agnes; and it proved to him that the rough pea-jacket of a man like Ham Peggotty might cover the simple heart of as honest a gentleman as ever lived.

THE BOY'S FATHER

The Boy, in his time, has been brought in contact with many famous men and women; but upon nothing in his whole experience does he look back now with greater satisfaction than upon his slight intercourse with the first great man he ever knew. Quite a little lad, he was staying at the Pulaski House in Savannah, in 1853 — perhaps it was in 1855 — when [p 57]

his father told him to observe particularly the old gentleman with the spectacles, who occupied a seat at their table in the public dining-room; for, he said, the time would come when The Boy would be very proud to say that he had breakfasted, and dined, and supped with Mr. Thackeray. He had no idea who, or what, Mr. Thackeray was; but his father considered him a great man, and that was enough for The Boy. He did pay particular attention to Mr. Thackeray, with his eyes and his ears; and one morning Mr. Thackeray paid a little attention to him, of which he is proud, indeed. Mr. Thackeray took The Boy between his knees, and asked his name, and what he intended to be when he grew up. He replied, "A farmer, sir." Why, he cannot imagine, for he never had the slightest inclination towards a farmer's life. And then Mr. Thackeray put his gentle hand upon The Boy's little red head, and said: "Whatever you are, try to be a good one."

To have been blessed by Thackeray is a distinction The Boy would not exchange for any niche in the Temple of Literary Fame; no laurel crown he could ever receive would be able to obliterate, or to equal, the sense of Thackeray's touch; and if there be any virtue in the laying on of hands The Boy can only hope that a little of it has descended upon him.

And whatever The Boy is, he has tried, for Thackeray's sake, "to be a good one!"

[p 59]
FOUR DOGS

[p 60]
WHISKIE
AN EAU DE VIE

In doggerel lines, Whiskie my dog I sing.
These lines are after Virgil, Pope, or some one.
His very voice has got a Whiskie Ring.
I call him Whiskie, 'cause he's such a rum one.

His is a high-whine, and his nip has power,
Hot-Scotch his temper, but no Punch is merrier;
Not Rye, not Schnappish, he's no Whiskie-Sour.
I call him Whiskie—he's a Whis-Skye terrier.

[p 61]
FOUR DOGS

It was Dr. John Brown, of Edinboro', who once spoke in sincere sympathy of the man who "led a dog-less life." It was Mr. "Josh Billings" who said that in the whole history of the world there is but one thing that money cannot buy, to wit: the wag of a dog's tail. And it was Professor John C. Van Dyke who declared the other day, in reviewing the artistic career of Landseer, that he made his dogs too human. It was the Great Creator himself who made dogs too human—so human that sometimes they put humanity to shame.

The Boy has been the friend and confidant of Four Dogs who have helped to humanize him for a quarter of a century and more, and who have souls to be saved, he is sure. And when he crosses the Stygian River he expects to find, on the other shore, a trio of dogs wagging their tails almost off, in their joy at his coming, and with honest tongues hanging out to lick his hands and his feet. And then he is [p 62]
going, with these faithful, devoted dogs at his heels, to talk about dogs with Dr. John Brown, Sir Edwin Landseer, and Mr. "Josh Billings."

The first dog, Whiskie, was an alleged Skye terrier, coming, alas! from a clouded, not a clear, sky. He had the most beautiful and the most perfect head ever seen on a dog, but his legs were altogether too long; and the rest of him, was—just dog. He came into the family in 1867 or 1868. He was, at the beginning, not popular with the seniors; but he was so honest, so ingenuous, so "square," that he made himself irresistible, and he soon became even dearer to the father and to the mother than he was to The Boy. Whiskie was not an amiable character, except to his own people. He hated everybody else, he barked at everybody else, and sometimes he bit everybody else—friends of the household as well as the butcher-boys, the baker-boys, and the borrowers of money who came to the door. He had no discrimination in his likes and dislikes, and, naturally, he was not popular, except among his own people. He hated all cats but his own cat, by whom he was bullied in a most outrageous way. Whiskie had the sense of shame and the sense of humor.

WHISKIE

One warm summer evening, the family was sitting on the front
steps, after a refreshing shower of rain, when Whiskie saw a cat in

the street, picking its dainty way among the little puddles of water.
With [p 63]
a muttered curse he dashed after the cat without discovering, until
within a few feet of it, that it was the cat who belonged to him. He
tried to stop himself in his impetuous career, he put on all his
brakes, literally skimming along the street railway-track as if he
were out simply for a slide, passing the cat, who gave him a half-
contemptuous, half-pitying look; and then, after inspecting the sky
to see if the rain was really over and how the wind was, he came
back to his place between the father and The Boy as if it were all a
matter of course and of every-day occurrence. But he knew they
were laughing at him; and if ever a dog felt sheepish, and looked
sheepish—if ever a dog said, "What an idiot I've made of myself!"
Whiskie was that dog.

The cat was a martinet in her way, and she demanded all the
privileges of her sex. Whiskie always gave her precedence, and once
when he, for a moment, forgot himself and started to go out of the
dining-room door before her, she deliberately slapped him in the
face; whereupon he drew back instantly, like the gentleman he was,
and waited for her to pass.

Whiskie was fourteen or fifteen years of age in 1882, when the
mother went to join the father, and The Boy was taken to Spain by a
good aunt and cousins. Whiskie was left at home to keep house
with the two old servants who had known him all his [p 64]
life, and were in perfect sympathy with him. He had often been left
alone before during the family's frequent journeyings about the
world, the entire establishment being kept running purely on his
account. Usually he did not mind the solitude; he was well taken
care of in their absence, and he felt that they were coming back
some day. This time he knew it was different. He would not be
consoled. He wandered listlessly and uselessly about the house; into
the mother's room, into his master's room; and one morning he was
found in a dark closet, where he had never gone before, dead—of a
broken heart.

He had only a stump of a tail, but he will wag it—when next his
master sees him!

PUNCH

The second dog was Punch—a perfect, thorough-bred Dandie Din-
mont, and the most intelligent, if not the most affectionate, of the
lot. Punch and The Boy kept house together for a year or two, and
alone. The first thing in the morning, the last thing at night, Punch
was in evidence. He went to the door to see his master safely off; he
was sniffing at the inside of the door the moment the key was heard
in the latch, no matter how late at night; and so long as there was
light enough he watched for his master out of the window. Punch,
too, had a cat—a son, or a grandson, of Whiskie's cat. Punch's favorite seat was in a chair in the front basement. Here, for hours, he
would look out at the passers-by—indulging [p 65]
in the study of man, the proper study of his kind. The chair was
what is known as "cane-bottomed," and through its perforations the
cat was fond of tickling Punch, as he sat. When Punch felt that the

joke had been carried far enough, he would rise in his wrath, chase the cat out into the kitchen, around the back-yard, into the kitchen again, and then, perhaps, have it out with the cat under the sink — without the loss of a hair, the use of a claw, or an angry spit or snarl. Punch and the cat slept together, and dined together, in utter harmony; and the master has often gone up to his own bed, after a solitary cigar, and left them purring and snoring in each other's arms. They assisted at each other's toilets, washed each other's faces, and once, when Mary Cook was asked what was the matter with Punch's eye, she said: "I *think*, Sur, that the cat must have put her finger in it, when she combed his bang!"
Punch loved everybody. He seldom barked, he never bit. He cared nothing for clothes, or style, or social position. He was as cordial to a beggar as he would have been to a king; and if thieves had come to break through and steal, Punch, in his unfailing, hospitable amiability, would have escorted them through the house, and shown them where the treasures were kept. All the children were fond of Punch, who accepted mauling as never did dog [p 66]
before. His master could carry him up-stairs by the tail, without a murmur of anything but satisfaction on Punch's part; and one favorite performance of theirs was an amateur representation of "Daniel in the Lion's Den," Punch being all the animals, his master, of course, being the prophet himself. The struggle for victory was something awful. Daniel seemed to be torn limb from limb, Punch, all the time, roaring like a thousand beasts of the forest, and treating his victim as tenderly as if he were wooing a sucking dove. The entertainment — when there were young persons at the house — was of nightly occurrence, and always repeatedly encored. Punch, however, never cared to play Lion to the Daniel of anybody else.

One of Punch's expressions of poetic affection is still preserved by a little girl who is now grown up, and has little girls of her own. It was attached to a Christmas-gift — a locket containing a scrap of blue-gray wool. And here it is:

> "Punch Hutton is ready to vow and declare
> That his friend Milly Barrett's a brick.
> He begs she'll accept of this lock of his hair;
> And he sends her his love — and a lick."

Punch's most memorable performance, perhaps, was his appearance at a dinner-party of little ladies and gentlemen. They were told
that the chief dish [p 67]
of the entertainment was one which they all particularly liked, and
their curiosity, naturally, was greatly excited. The table was cleared,
the carving-knife was sharpened in a most demonstrative manner,
and half a dozen pairs of very wide-open little eyes were fixed upon
the door through which the waitress entered, bearing aloft an
enormous platter, upon which nothing was visible but a cover of
equally enormous size — both of them borrowed, by-the-way, for the
important occasion. When the cover was raised, with all ceremony,
Punch was discovered, in a highly nervous state, and apparently as
much delighted and amused at the situation as was anybody else.
The guests, with one voice, declared that he was "sweet enough to
eat."

Punch died very suddenly; poisoned, it is supposed, by somebody whom he never injured. He never injured a living soul! And
when Mary Cook dug a hole, by the side of Whiskie's grave, one
raw afternoon, and put Punch into it, his master is not ashamed to
confess that he shut himself up in his room, threw himself onto the
bed, and cried as he has not cried since they took his mother away
from him.

Mop was the third of the quartet of dogs, and he came into the
household like the Quality of Mercy. A night or two after the death
of Punch, his master chanced to be dining with the Coverleys, in [p
68]
Brooklyn. Mr. Coverley, noticing the trappings and the suits of woe
which his friend wore in his face, naturally asked the cause. He had
in his stable a Dandie as fine as Punch, whom he had not seen, or
thought of, for a month. Would the bereaved one like to see him?
The mourner would like to look at any dog who looked like the
companion who had been taken from him; and a call, through a
speaking-tube, brought into the room, head over heels, with all the
wild impetuosity of his race, Punch personified, his ghost embod-
ied, his twin brother. The same long, lithe body, the same short legs
(the fore legs shaped like a capital S), the same short tail, the same
hair dragging the ground, the same beautiful head, the same wist-
ful, expressive eye, the same cool, insinuating nose. The new-comer

raced around the table, passing his owner unnoticed, and not a word was spoken. Then this Dandie cut a sort of double pigeon-wing, gave a short bark, put his crooked, dirty little feet on the stranger's knees, insinuated his cool and expressive nose into an unresisting hand, and wagged his stump of a tail with all his loving might. It was the longed-for touch of a vanished paw, the lick of a tongue that was still. He was unkempt, uncombed, uncared for, but he was another Punch, and he knew a friend when he saw one. "If that were my dog he would not live forgotten in a stable: he would take the place in the society to which his [p 69]
birth and his evident breeding entitle him," was the friend's remark, and Mop regretfully went back to his stall.

MOP AND HIS MASTER

The next morning, early, he came into the Thirty-fourth Street study, combed, kempt, shining, cared for to a superlative degree; with a note in his mouth signifying that his name was Mop and that he was The Boy's. He was The Boy's, and The Boy was his, so long as he lived, ten happy years for both of them.

Without Punch's phenomenal intelligence, Mop had many of Punch's ways, and all of Punch's trust and affection; and, like Punch, he was never so superlatively happy as when he was roughly mauled and pulled about by his tail. When by chance he was shut out in the back-yard, he knocked, with his tail, on the door; he squirmed his way into the heart of Mary Cook in the first ten minutes, and in half an hour he was on terms of the most affectionate friendship with Punch's cat.

Mop had absolutely no sense of fear or of animal proportions. As a catter he was never equalled; a Yale-man, by virtue of an honorary degree, he tackled everything he ever met in the feline way — with the exception of the Princeton Tiger — and he has been known to attack dogs seven times as big as himself. He learned nothing by experience: he never knew when he was thrashed. The butcher's dog at [p 70]
Onteora whipped, and bit, and chewed him into semi-helpless unconsciousness three times a week for four months, one summer; and yet Mop, half paralyzed, bandaged, soaked in Pond's Extract, unable to hold up his head to respond to the greetings of his own family, speechless for hours, was up and about and ready for another fray and another chewing, the moment the butcher's dog, unseen, unscented by the rest of the household, appeared over the brow of the hill.

The only creature by whom Mop was ever really overcome was a black-and-white, common, every-day, garden skunk. He treed this unexpected visitor on the wood-pile one famous moonlight night in Onteora. And he acknowledged his defeat at once, and like a man. He realized fully his own unsavory condition. He retired to a far corner of the small estate, and for a week, prompted only by his own instinct, he kept to the leeward of Onteora society.

He went out of Onteora, that summer, in a blaze of pugnacious glory. It was the last day of the season; many households were being broken up, and four or five families were leaving the colony together. All was confusion and hurry at the little railway station at Tannersville. Scores of trunks were being checked, scores of packages were being labelled for expressage, every hand held a bag, or a bundle, or both; and Mop, a semi-invalid, his fore paw [p 71] and his ear in slings, the result of recent encounters with the butcher's dog, was carried, for safety's sake, and for the sake of his own comfort, in a basket, which served as an ambulance, and was carefully placed in the lap of the cook. As the train finally started, already ten minutes late, the cook, to give her hero a last look at the Hill-of-the-Sky, opened the basket, and the window, that he might wag a farewell tail. When lo! the butcher's dog appeared upon the scene, and, in an instant, Mop was out of the window and under the car-wheels, in the grip of the butcher's dog. Intense was the excitement. The engine was stopped, and brakemen, and firemen, and conductors, and passengers, and on-lookers, and other dogs, were shouting and barking and trying to separate the combatants. At the end of a second ten minutes Mop — minus a piece of the other ear — was back in his ambulance: conquered, but happy. He never saw the butcher's dog or Onteora again.

To go back a little. Mop was the first person who was told of his master's engagement, and he was the first to greet the wife when she came home, a bride, to his own house. He had been made to understand, from the beginning, that she did not care for dogs — in general. And he set himself out to please, and to overcome the unspoken antagonism. He had a delicate part to play, and he played it with a delicacy and a tact which rarely have been equalled. He did [p 72] not assert himself; he kept himself in the background; he said little; his approaches at first were slight and almost imperceptible, but he was always ready to do, or to help, in an unaggressive way. He followed her about the house, up-stairs and down-stairs, and he looked and waited. Then he began to sit on the train of her gown; to stand as close to her as was fit and proper; once in a while to jump upon the sofa beside her, or into the easy-chair behind her, winking at his master, from time to time, in his quiet way.

And at last he was successful. One dreary winter, when he suffered terribly from inflammatory rheumatism, he found his mistress making a bed for him by the kitchen fire, getting up in the middle of the night to go down to look after him, when he uttered, in pain, the cries he could not help. And when a bottle of very rare old brandy, kept for some extraordinary occasion of festivity, was missing, the master was informed that it had been used in rubbing Mop!

Mop's early personal history was never known. Told once that he was the purest Dandie in America, and asked his pedigree, his master was moved to look into the matter of his family tree. It seems that a certain sea-captain was commissioned to bring back to this country the best Dandie to be had in all Scotland. He sent his quartermaster to find him, and [p 73]
the quartermaster found Mop under a private carriage, in Argyle Street, Glasgow, and brought him on board. That is Mop's pedigree.

Mop died of old age and of a complication of diseases, in the spring of 1892. He lost his hair, he lost his teeth, he lost everything but his indomitable spirit; and when almost on the brink of the grave, he stood in the back-yard — literally, on the brink of his own grave — for eight hours in a March snow-storm, motionless, and watching a great black cat on the fence, whom he hypnotized, and who finally came down to be killed. The cat weighed more than Mop did, and was very gamy. And the encounter nearly cost a lawsuit.

This was Mop's last public appearance. He retired to his bed before the kitchen range, and gradually and slowly he faded away: amiable, unrepining, devoted to the end. A consultation of doctors showed that his case was hopeless, and Mop was condemned to be carried off to be killed humanely by the society founded by Mr. Bergh, where without cruelty they end the sufferings of animals. Mop had not left his couch for weeks. His master spoke to him about it, with tears in his eyes, one night. He said: "To-morrow must end it, old friend. 'Tis for your sake and your relief. It almost breaks my heart, old friend. But there is another and a better world — even for dogs, old friend. And for old [p 74]
acquaintance' sake, and for old friendship's sake, I must have you sent on ahead of me, old friend."

The next morning, when he came down to breakfast, there by the empty chair sat Mop. How he got himself up the stairs nobody knows. But there he was, and the society which a good man founded saw not Mop that day.

The end came soon afterwards. And Mop has gone on to join Whiskie and Punch in their waiting for The Boy.

The family went abroad for a year's stay, when Mop died, and they rented the house to good people and good tenants, who have never been forgiven for one particular act. They buried a dog of their own in the family plot in the back-yard, and under the ailantus-tree which shades the graves of the cats and the dogs; and The Boy feels that they have profaned the spot!

It seemed to his master, after the passing of Mop, that the master's earthly account with dogs was closed. The pain of parting was too great to be endured. But another Dandie came to him, one Christmas morning, to fill the aching void; and for a time again his life is not a dogless one.

ROY AND HIS MASTER

The present ruler of the household has a pedigree much longer and much straighter than his own front legs. Although he comes from a distinguished line of prize-winning thoroughbreds, he never will be

[p 75]

permitted to compete for a medal on his own behalf. The Dog Show should be suppressed by the Society for the Prevention of Cruelty to Dogs. It has ruined the dispositions and broken the hearts of very many of the best friends humanity ever had. And the man who would send his dog to the Dog Show, would send his wife to a Wife Show, and permit his baby to be exhibited, in public, for a blue ribbon or a certificate — at an admission-fee of fifty cents a head!

Mop's successor answers to the name of Roy — when he answers to anything at all. He is young, very wilful, and a little hard of hearing, of which latter affliction he makes the most. He always understands when he is invited to go out. He is stone-deaf, invariably, when he is told to come back. But he is full of affection, and he has a keen sense of humor. In the face he looks like Thomas Carlyle, and Professor John Weir declares that his body is all out of drawing!

At times his devotion to his mistress is beautiful and touching. It is another case of "Mary and the Lamb, you know." If his mistress is not visible, he waits patiently about; and he is sure to go wherever she goes. It makes the children of the neighborhood laugh and play. But it is severe upon the master, who does most of the training, while the mistress gets most of the devotion. That is the way with lambs, and with dogs, and with some folks!

[p 76]
Roy is quite as much of a fighter as was any one of the other dogs; but he is a little more discriminating in his likes and his dislikes. He fights all the dogs in Tannersville; he fights the Drislers' Gyp almost every time he meets him; he fights the Beckwiths' Blennie only when either one of them trespasses on the domestic porch of the other (Blennie, who is very pretty, looks like old portraits of Mrs. Browning, with the curls hanging on each side of the face); and Roy never fights Laddie Pruyn nor Jack Ropes at all. Jack Ropes is the hero whom he worships, the beau ideal to him of everything a dog should be. He follows Jack in all respects; and he pays Jack the sincere flattery of imitation. Jack, an Irish setter, is a thorough gentleman in form, in action, and in thought. Some years Roy's senior, he submits patiently to the playful capers of the younger dog; and he even accepts little nips at his legs or his ears. It is pleasant to watch the two friends during an afternoon walk. Whatever Jack does, that does Roy; and Jack knows it, and he gives Roy hard things to do. He

leads Roy to the summit of high rocks, and then he jumps down, realizing that Roy is too small to take the leap. But he always waits until Roy, yelping with mortification, comes back by the way they both went. He wades through puddles up to his own knees, but over Roy's head; and then he trots cheerfully away, far in advance, while Roy has [p 77]
to stop long enough to shake himself dry. But it was Roy's turn once! He traversed a long and not very clean drain, which was just large enough to give free passage to his own small body; and Jack went rushing after. Jack got through; but he was a spectacle to behold. And there are creditable eye-witnesses who are ready to testify that Roy took Jack home, and sat on the steps, and laughed, while Jack was being washed.

ROY

Each laughed on the wrong side of his mouth, however—Jack from agony, and Roy from sympathy—when Jack, a little later, had his unfortunate adventure with the loose-quilled, fretful, Onteora porcupine. It nearly cost Jack his life and his reason; and for some time he was a helpless, suffering invalid. Doctors were called in, chloroform was administered, and many delicate surgical operations were performed before Jack was on his feet again; and for the while each tail drooped. Happily for Roy, he did not go to the top of the Hill-of-the-Sky that unlucky day, and so he escaped the porcupine. But Roy does not care much for porcupines, anyway, and he never did. Other dogs are porcupiney enough for him!

Roy's association with Jack Ropes is a liberal education to him in more ways than one. Jack is so big and so strong and so brave, and so gentle withal, and so refined in manners and intellectual in mind, that Roy, even if he would, could not resist the healthful [p 78] influence. Jack never quarrels except when Roy quarrels; and whether Roy is in the right or in the wrong, the aggressor or the attacked (and generally he begins it), Jack invariably interferes on Roy's behalf, in a good-natured, big-brother, what-a-bother sort of way that will not permit Roy to be the under dog in any fight. Part of Roy's dislike of Blennie—Blennie is short for Blenheim—consists in the fact that while Blennie is nice enough in his way, it is not Roy's way. Blennie likes to sit on laps, to bark out of windows—at a safe distance. He wears a little sleigh-bell on his collar. Under no circumstances does he play follow-my-leader, as Jack does. He does not try to do stunts; and, above all, he does not care to go in swimming.

The greatest event, perhaps, in Roy's young life was his first swim. He did not know he could swim. He did not know what it was to swim. He had never seen a sheet of water larger than a road-side puddle or than the stationary wash-tubs of his own laundry at home. He would have nothing to do with the Pond, at first, except for drinking purposes; and he would not enter the water until Jack went in, and then nothing would induce him to come out of the water—until Jack was tired. His surprise and his pride at being able to take care of himself in an entirely unknown and unexplored element were very great. But—there is always a *But* in Roy's case—but [p 79] when he swam ashore the trouble began. Jack, in a truly Chesterfieldian manner, dried himself in the long grass on the banks. Roy dried *him*self in the deep yellow dust of the road—a medium which was quicker and more effective, no doubt, but not so pleasant for those about him; for he was so enthusiastic over his performance that he jumped upon everybody's knickerbockers, or upon the skirts of everybody's gown, for the sake of a lick at somebody's hand and a pat of appreciation and applause.

Another startling and never-to-be-forgotten experience of Roy's was his introduction to the partridge. He met the partridge casually one afternoon in the woods, and he paid no particular attention to it. He looked upon it as a plain barn-yard chicken a little out of place; but when the partridge whirled and whizzed and boomed itself into the air, Roy put all his feet together, and jumped, like a bucking horse, at the lowest estimate four times as high as his own head. He thought it was a porcupine! He had heard a great deal about porcupines, although he had never seen one; and he fancied that that was the way porcupines always went off!

Roy likes and picks blackberries—the green as well as the ripe; and he does not mind having his portrait painted. Mr. Beckwith considers Roy one of the best models he ever had. Roy does not have to be posed; he poses himself, willingly and patiently, [p 80]
so long as he can pose himself very close to his master; and he always places his front legs, which he knows to be his strong point, in the immediate foreground. He tries very hard to look pleasant, as if he saw a chipmunk at the foot of a tree, or as if he thought Mr. Beckwith was squeezing little worms of white paint out of little tubes just for his amusement. And if he really does see a chipmunk on a stump, he rushes off to bark at the chipmunk; and then he comes back and resumes his original position, and waits for Mr. Beckwith to go on painting again. Once in awhile, when he feels that Mr. Beckwith has made a peculiarly happy remark, or an unusually happy stroke of the brush, Roy applauds tumultuously and loudly with his tail, against the seat of the bench or the side of the house. Roy has two distinct wags—the perpendicular and the horizontal; and in his many moments of enthusiasm he never neglects to use that particular wag which is likely to make the most noise.

"HE TRIES VERY HARD TO LOOK PLEASANT"

Roy has many tastes and feelings which are in entire sympathy with those of his master. He cannot get out of a hammock unless he falls out; and he is never so miserable as when Mrs. Butts comes over from the Eastkill Valley to clean house. Mrs. Butts piles all the sitting-room furniture on the front piazza, and then she scrubs the sitting-room floor, and neither Roy nor his master, so long as Mrs. Butts [p 81]
has control, can enter the sitting-room for a bone or a book. And they do not like it, although they like Mrs. Butts.

Roy has his faults; but his evil, as a rule, is wrought by want of thought rather than by want of heart. He shows his affection for his friends by walking under their feet and getting his own feet stepped on, or by sitting so close to their chairs that they rock on his tail. He has been known to hold two persons literally spellbound for minutes, with his tail under the rocker of one chair and both ears under the rocker of another one. Roy's greatest faults are barking at horses' heels and running away. This last is very serious, and often it is annoying; but there is always some excuse for it. He generally runs away to the Williamsons', which is the summer home of his John and his Sarah; and where lodges Miss Flossie Burns, of Tannersville, his summer-girl. He knows that the Williamsons themselves do not want too much of him, no matter how John and Sarah and Miss Burns may feel on the subject; and he knows, too, that his

own family wishes him to stay more at home; but, for all that, he runs away. He slips off at every opportunity. He pretends that he is only going down to the road to see what time it is, or that he is simply setting out for a blackberry or the afternoon's mail; and when he is brought reluctantly home, he makes believe that he has
[p 82]
forgotten all about it; and he naps on the top step, or in the doorway, in the most guileless and natural manner; and then, when nobody is looking, he dashes off, barking at any imaginary ox-cart, in wild, unrestrainable impetuosity, generally in the direction of the Williamsons' cottage, and bringing up, almost invariably, under the Williamsons' kitchen stove.

He would rather be shut up, in the Williamsons' kitchen, with John and Sarah, and with a chance of seeing Flossie through the wire-screened door, than roam in perfect freedom over all his own domain.

He will bark at horses' heels until he is brought home, some day, with broken ribs. Nothing but hard experience teaches Roy. There is no use of boxing his ears. That only hurts his feelings, and gives him an extra craving for sympathy. He licks the hand that licks him, until everyone of the five fingers is heartily ashamed of itself.

"He is stone-deaf when he is asked to come back"   "He pretends he has for

"He poses willingly and steadily"
ROY

"He waits patiently a`

Several autograph letters of Roy's, in verse, in blank-verse, and in plain, hard prose, signed by his own mark—a fore paw dipped in an ink-bottle and stamped upon the paper—were sold by Mrs. Custer at varying prices during a fair for the benefit of the Onteora Chapel Fund, in 1896.

To one friend he wrote:

> "My dear Blennie Beckwith,—You are a sneak; and a snip; and a snide; and a snob; and a snoozer; and a snarler; and a snapper; and a skunk. And I hate you; and I loathe you; [p 83]
> and I despise you; and I abominate you; and I scorn you; and I repudiate you; and I abhor you; and I dislike you; and I eschew you; and I dash you; and I dare you.
>
> "Your affectionate friend,
>
> "P. S.—I've licked this spot.
>
> "R. H.
>
> His

Roy  Hutton.

mark.

"Witness: Kate Lynch."

Inspired by Miss Flossie Williamson Burns's bright eyes, he dropped into poetry in addressing her:

> "Say I'm barkey; say I'm bad;
> Say the Thurber pony kicked me;
> Say I run away — but add —
> 'Flossie licked me.'

his

"Witness: Sarah Johnson." "Roy × Hutton.
mark.

In honor of "John Ropes, Esquire," he went to Shakspere:

[p 84]
"But that I am forbid
To tell the secrets of thy mountain climb,
I could a tail unfold, whose lightest wag
Would harrow up the roof of thy mouth, draw thy
young blood,

Make thy two eyes, like a couple of safety-matches,
start from their spheres;
Thy knotted and combined locks to part right
straight down the middle of thy back,
And each particular brick-red hair to stand on end
Full of quills, shot out by a fretful Onteora porcu-
pine.
But this eternal blazon must not be
To ears that are quite as handsome as is the rest of
thy beautiful body.

    ("'Hamlet,' altered to suit, by)

<table>
<tr><td></td><td></td><td>his</td></tr>
<tr><td>"Witness: John Johnson."</td><td></td><td>"Roy × Hutton.</td></tr>
<tr><td></td><td></td><td>mark.</td></tr>
</table>

His latest poetical effort was the result of his affection for a Scottish collie, in his neighborhood, and was indited

TO LADDIE PRUYN, ESQ.

Should Auld Acquaintance be forgot,
And the Dogs of Auld Lang Syne?
I'll wag a tail o' kindness yet,
For the sake of Auld Ladd Pruyn.
Witnesses:
Marion Lyman,
Effie Waddington,
Katherine Lyman.

THE WAITING THREE

While Roy was visiting the Fitches and the Telford children, and little Agnes Ogden, at Wilton, Conn., some time afterwards, he dictated a long letter to his master, some portions of which, perhaps, [p 85]
are worth preserving. After the usual remarks upon the weather and the general health of the family, he touched upon serious, personal matters which had evidently caused him some mental and physical uneasiness. And he explained that while he was willing to confess that he *did* chase the white cat into a tree, and keep her away from her kittens for a couple of hours, he *did not* kill the little chicken. The little chicken, stepped upon by its own mother, was dead, quite dead, when he picked it up, and brought it to the house. And he made Dick Fitch, who was an eye-witness to the whole transaction, add a post-script testifying that the statement was true.

John says the letter sounds exactly like Roy!

Roy's is a complex character. There is little medium about Roy. He is very good when he is good, and he is very horrid indeed when he is bad. He is a strange admixture of absolute devotion and of utter inconstancy. Nothing will entice him away from John on one day, neither threats nor persuasion. The next day he will cut John dead in the road, with no sign of recognition. He sees John, and he goes slowly and deliberately out of his way to pass John by, without a look or a sniff. He comes up-stairs every morning when his master's shaving-water is produced. He watches intently the entire course of his master's toilet; he follows his master, step by step, from bed to bureau, from closet to [p 86]
chair; he lies across his master's feet; he minds no sprinkling from his master's sponge, so anxious is he that his master shall not slip away, and go to his breakfast without him. And then, before his master is ready to start, Roy goes off to breakfast, alone — at the Williamsons'! He will torment his master sometimes for hours to be taken out to walk; he will interrupt his master's work, disturb his master's afternoon nap, and refuse all invitations to run away for a walk on his own account. And the moment he and his master have started, he will join the first absolute stranger he meets, and walk off with that stranger in the opposite direction, and in the most confidential manner possible!

There are days when he will do everything he should do, everything he is told to do, everything he is wanted to do. There are days and days together when he does nothing that is right, when he is disobedient, disrespectful, disobliging, disagreeable, even disreputable. And all this on purpose!

It is hard to know what to do with Roy: how to treat him; how to bring him up. He may improve as he grows older. Perhaps to his unfortunate infirmity may be ascribed his uncertainty and his variability of temper and disposition. It is possible that he cannot hear even when he wants to hear. It is not impossible that he is making-believe all the time. One great, good thing can be said for Roy: he is
[p 87]
never really cross; he never snaps; he never snarls; he never bites his human friends, no matter how great the provocation may be. Roy is a canine enigma, the most eccentric of characters. His family cannot determine whether he is a gump or a genius. But they know he is nice; and they like him!

Long may Roy be spared to wag his earthly tail, and to bay deep-mouthed welcome to his own particular people as they draw near home. How the three dogs who have gone on ahead agree now with each other, and how they will agree with Roy, no man can say. They did not agree with very many dogs in this world. But that they are waiting together, all three of them, for Roy and for The Boy, and in perfect harmony, The Boy is absolutely sure.

MOP